# PENCIL'S PERFECT PICTURE

**Jodi McKay**          illustrated by **Juliana Motzko**

Albert Whitman & Company
Chicago, Illinois

For my husband, J, who thinks everything I do is perfect. Right? Love—JMcK

To my family, for all of their love and support to me and my artistic journey—JM

Library of Congress Cataloging-in-Publication data is on file with the publisher.

Text copyright © 2019 by Jodi McKay
Illustrations copyright © 2019 by Albert Whitman & Company
Illustrated by Juliana Motzko
First published in the United States of America in 2019 by Albert Whitman & Company
ISBN 978-0-8075-6476-9

Printed in China
10 9 8 7 6 5 4 3 2 1 HH 22 21 20 19

Design by Aphee Messer and Anahid Hamparian

For more information about Albert Whitman & Company,
visit our website at www.albertwhitman.com.

100 Years of Albert Whitman & Company
Celebrate with us in 2019!

I want to do something special for my dad today.
But what?

I know! I'll draw him the greatest, the best, the most
perfect picture he has ever seen!

There's just one problem;
I don't know what makes a picture perfect.
Hmm.

I'll have to learn what a perfect picture looks like before I can draw one, and I think I know where to find the answer.

Swish,

Swash.

Swoosh.

Voilà!

Incredible! It looks so real.

Does that make your picture perfect?

Perfect? Pah! I paint for pleasure.

That's nice, but I have to know what makes a picture perfect.

I'll ask Marker. Maybe I can catch a tip or two from him.

Hi, Marker. You know a lot about drawing, right?

Absolutely!

First, I draw over here.

Next, I move straight up the side,

and then I circle back home for the win!

Wow! Such action!

Does that make your picture perfect?

Perfect schmerfect! My motto is, "Do your best."

That's a great goal. I'm doing my best
to find out how to make a perfect picture.

I'll go ask Pastel. She may have the answer I need.

And now create!

Beautiful! Your picture makes me feel happy.

Would you say that makes it perfect?

I draw for peace, not perfection.

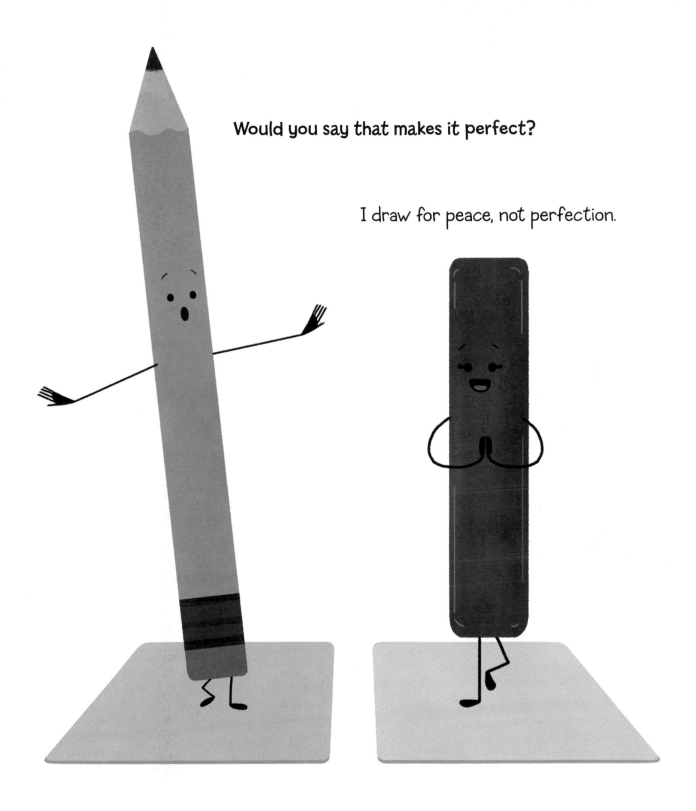

I don't think I'll find peace until I know how to draw a perfect picture.
I bet the crayons know. They really think outside the box.

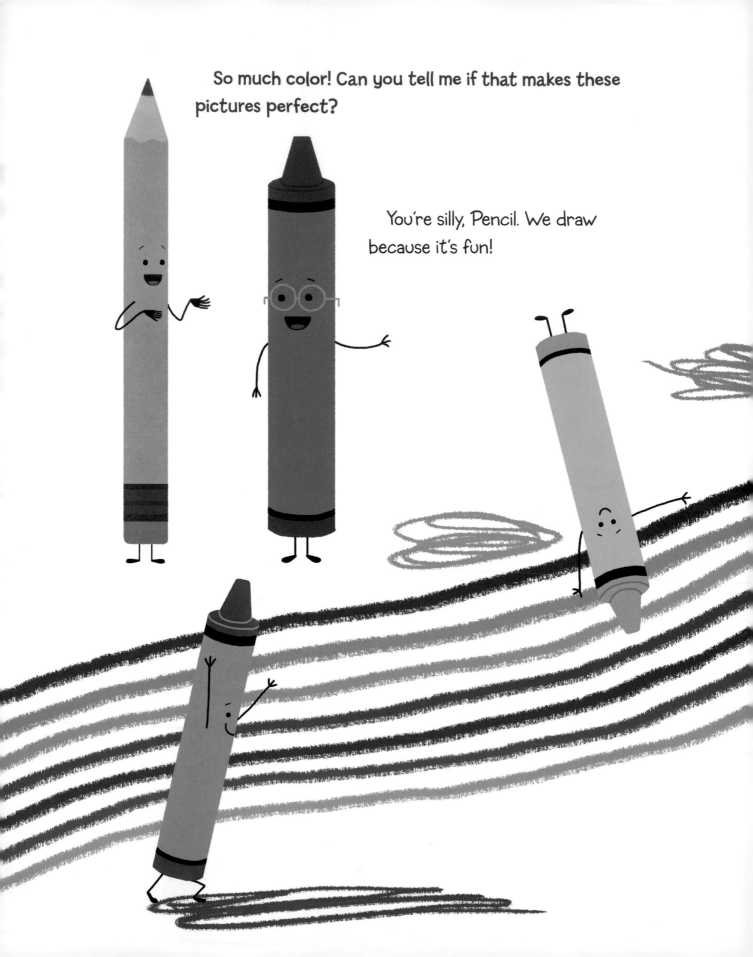

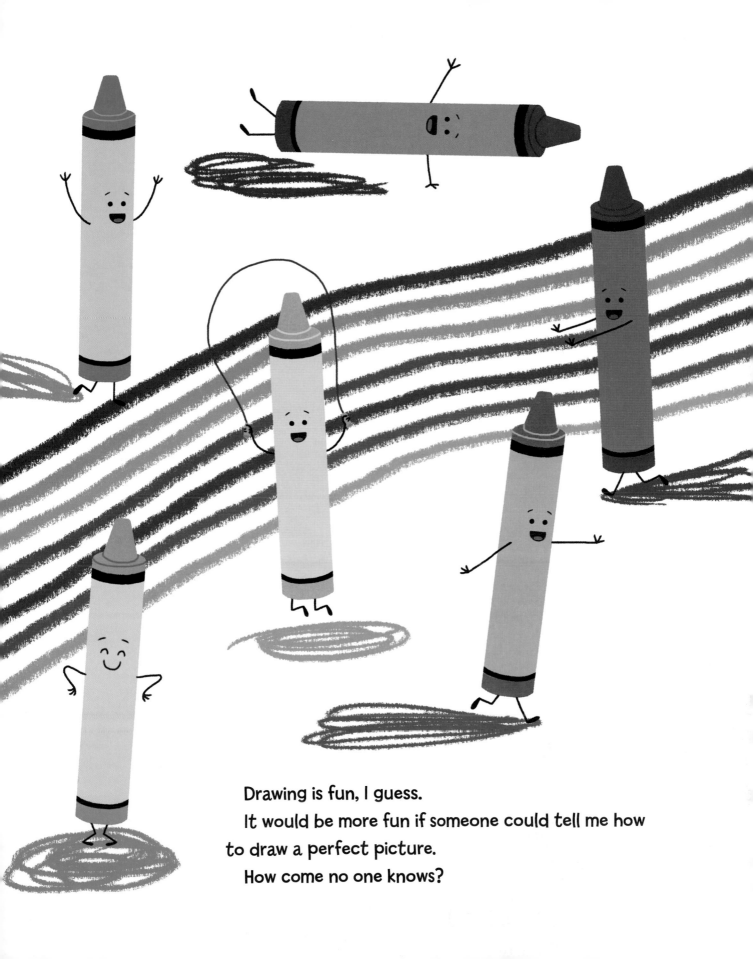

Drawing is fun, I guess.

It would be more fun if someone could tell me how to draw a perfect picture.

How come no one knows?

**Squeak!**

Oh, hey Chalk. That's quite a picture you have there.

It's noisy, yet nice. Does that make it a perfect picture?

OH, HI PENCIL!
DID YOU SAY SOMETHING?

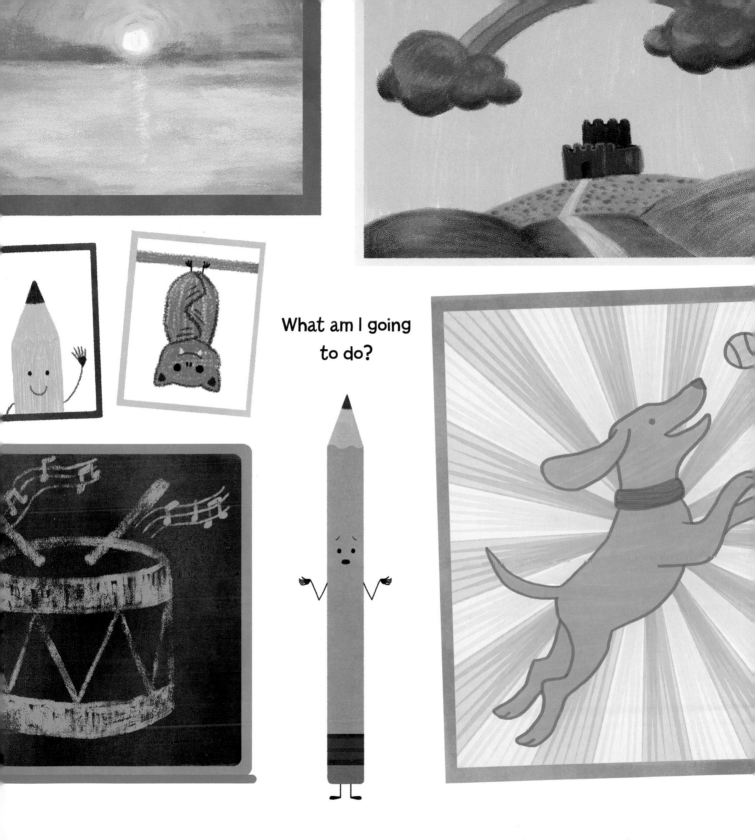

What am I going to do?

I want to draw a beautiful, incredible, positively perfect picture for my dad, but I still don't know what makes a picture perfect.

All I learned was to draw for pleasure or peace,

to have fun,

and to do my best.

Wait! What if I put them together...

*Scritch.*

Circle back here.

*Scratch.*

Breathe in...Blow it out....

*Scribble.*

Woo-hoo! This *is* fun!

Did I do it? Is this a perfect picture?

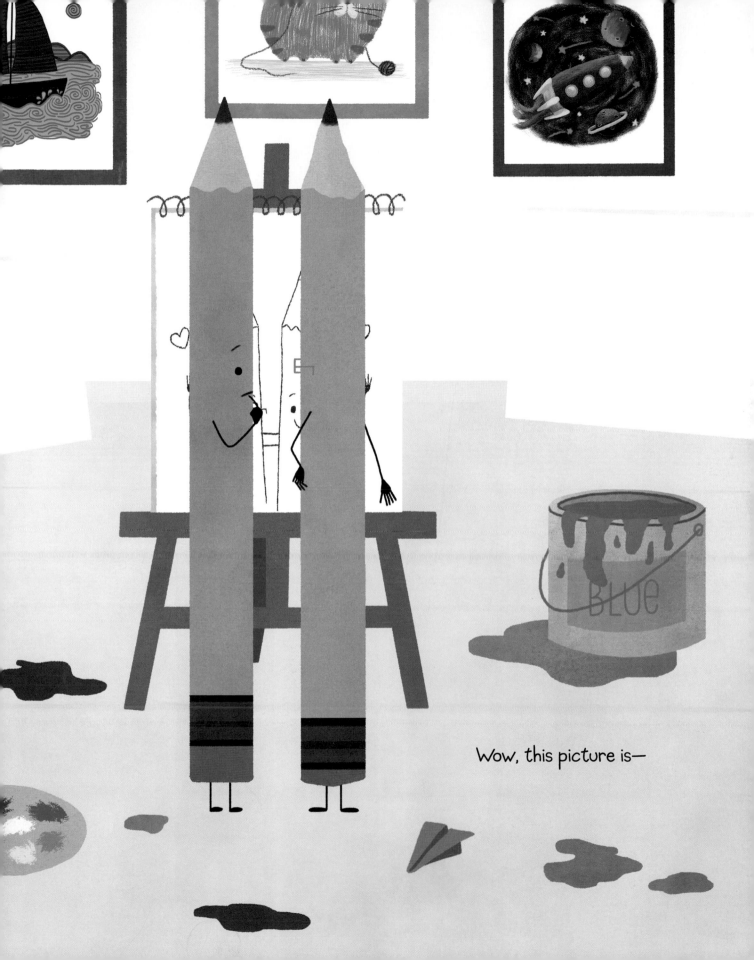

Wow, this picture is—

PERFECT!

Really?
But how do you know?

It's perfect because YOU drew it for me.